The Elk in the Glade

The World of Pioneer and Painter Jennie Hicks

Bruce E. Whitacre

Crown Rock Media

Forest Hills, New York

The Elk in the Glade: The World of Pioneer and Painter Jennie Hicks

Copyright © 2022 by Bruce E. Whitacre

All rights reserved. Except for use in any review or for educational purposes, the reproduction or utilization of this work, in whole or in part in any form by electronic, mechanical, or other means now known or hereafter invented, including xerography, photocopying, and recording, or in any information or retrieval system, is forbidden without the written permission of the publisher.

Crown Rock Media
Forest Hills, NY
www.crownrockmedia.com

First North American Publication 2022

Library of Congress Control Number: 202294509

ISBN 978-1-946116-25-3 (paperback)
ISBN 978-1-946116-26-0 (ebook)

Photo of Jennie Hicks, reprinted with permission of *The North Platte Telegraph*, taken by staff photographer, 1957

Cover art: Jennie Hicks, *The Elk in the Glade*, c.1930, oil on canvas, 23 in. x 17.5 in., Collection of Kent and Theresa Whitacre

Author photo: Federico Pestilli

Publisher's Cataloging-in-Publication data

Names: Whitacre, Bruce, author.
Title: The elk in the glade : the world of pioneer and painter Jennie Hicks / Bruce E. Whitacre.
Description: New York, NY: Crown Rock Media, 2022.
Identifiers:
LCCN: 2022945093 | ISBN: 978-1-946116-25-3 (paperback) | 978-1-946116-26-0 (ebook)
Subjects: LCSH Hicks, Jennie, 1879-1977--Poetry. | Artists--Poetry. | Artists--Biography. | Painters--Poetry. | Painters--Biography. | Artists--Nebraska--Biography. | BISAC POETRY / Subjects & Themes / Family | BIOGRAPHY & AUTOBIOGRAPHY / Artists, Architects, Photographers | ART / Folk & Outsider Art
Classification: LCC PS3623.H5628 E55 2022 | DDC 811--dc23

Jennie Hicks, 1957, courtesy of *North Platte Telegraph*

Contents

Introduction

"I will now tell about my hobby . . ."

Thus Jennie described her remarkable career as a landscape painter, working and selling her paintings out of her tiny Farnam, Nebraska home for over thirty years. This book is inspired by the many stories I heard growing up, told by Jennie and her daughters, who thrived on the Hi-Line, a string of towns along Highway 23 in southwest Nebraska. Their lives, mostly in the twentieth century, spanned horse power to nuclear power, boom and bust, war and peace. They knew people who had fought the Civil War, and a couple of them lived to watch 9/11 on television.

In putting these stories down on paper, yes, I have taken some liberties. I have also sometimes felt a guiding hand, a muted whisper, a shaking head, a presence that endures, as all our dead do. And so the conversation continues.

Jennie Hicks, after Herbert Herget, *The Horse Trader*, circa 1936.
Oil on canvas, 20.5 × 29.5 in. Author's collection.

Small White House in the Small Town

Small white house in the small town
on the Hi-Line.
Jennie tells how Horace, her father, dug the first well.
They came out from Ohio betting on hope.
Because Father was a carpenter
the soddy had rare wood-framed windows,
windows battered hard in '88.
Blizzards were a fact of life in
Farnham, Moorefield, Curtis, Maywood, and beyond,
the small towns of the Hi-Line.

Left her heart back in Ohio—first her favorite brother,
then a lover . . .

Returned to Nebraska, the Hi-Line.
Married old and had three girls:
Esther, Dorathy, and Ruth.
But it was Ohio where she learned to paint oils.

Painted everything that was not Hi-Line:
purple mountains, blue lakes, green trees,
elk, lions, sailboats, stones, cottages nestled,
copied from calendars, postcards, magazines,
then sold for a few dollars to view-starved farmers
          and their wives on the brown prairies.

She doesn't tell how
husband killed, farming—not even sixty—
just as he got off his knees from '29.
After one farm gone, him dead, last farm sold,
she moved into the small white house in the small town.

A house too cold for winters,
so she migrated among those daughters
          and their silent husbands.
Couldn't wait to return across the Hi-Line,
home to the small white house in the small town

each spring and open the studio in the pantry.
Smock and paint tubes, canvases,
the smell of baking bread and turpentine,
a dwindling paradise as friends die off,
dumping autumn ashes on the daffodils,
daughters getting older.
Sons-in-law suffer her still.
Home is the small white house in the small town.

Paintings hung in homes across the land,
a Nebraska Grandma Moses
telling tales to children.
Now almost deaf to their voices
she gazes out the south window.
Her brown eyes assay the light.
Sun sets and splits on the blade
        of the Hi-Line.
Farnham, Moorefield, Curtis, Maywood, and beyond . . .
the small white house in the small town.

Jennie at Thanksgiving

The family sedan purrs down the long lane that traces
a creek bed sprinkled with plum and cedar until it eases through
a pass in the clay banks and settles in the cozy farmstead of
Aunt Ruth and Uncle Glen:
neat, two-story house with garden, a big white barn, corrals
nestled in a valley like a little village.
I slip through the steamy kitchen,
where the women wrestle the bird
and lay out the Jell-O salads for dessert,
to the shadowy living room.
Men are talking prices and sports in halting mumbles.
And there, in a corner in the good chair, she sits:
angular jaw, crepe-skinned, permed white hair,
“hard-of-hearing”
Jennie.

She smiles her three-toothed grin
and extends her bony blue arms.
I take my place beside her.
Her large mountain lake painting
seems to cover the wall opposite, above the TV.
Her voice is soft, with a lot of tongue slipping between her lips.

Her dark, bright eyes, mirrored in all three daughters,
glisten as I ask and listen.
She loves to tell. She grows younger in telling
about blizzards, sod houses, wagons fording the river,
until we are called to the long table in the narrow room.

After a short prayer the endless passing begins:
turkey, dressing, potatoes, gravy, green beans, mystery casserole,
sweet potatoes, cranberry in ruby disks, until finally
it has all gone all around and we can eat.
Jennie gets hers ground to mush.
She gums away fitfully.
She can't hear anything in the din.
It will soon be time for her nap.
Time for seconds and again the rite of passing,
then dessert. It is endless.
I look around the table at four generations gathered.
It seems it will always be so.

The White Crib

1882
The journey began with a white crib,
a cage, a case, a conveyance,
one April night in Cleveland when
the uncles carried the orphan Jennie in her crib
down the street to the aunt
waiting in a shawl at the door.
"Up to the left. It's cold. What can I do?"
The brown-haired girl with glowing eyes, barely three,
wrapped her fat knuckles around the white dowels.
She would cling to those dowels, her only home,
peering out at the unfamiliar family,
her gaze sometimes peculiar with
her thoughts even then as she waited
for her father, Horace, to remarry.

1884
Now the white crib rides in a freight car,
following the fuming locomotive
and the bright-eyed girl west across two great rivers
and along a third, the Platte.

Her new mother, Mary, has not smiled since Chicago,
but no woman was ever a willing pioneer.
Father gave up trying to convince her this was a good idea,
but here she is anyway,
too many boys and this girl
and one more headed for that crib back there.
Mary gazes balefully at the treeless, blank plain.
"At least we'd see any savages a long way off," she grumbles.
Jennie pictures an arrowhead buried in Mary's furrowed brow.
Her dark hair has almost escaped its braids;
it has been a restless ride.
The boys squeal and tease. The girl whines for candy;
Mary pops her bottom with a pretty hand.
"You can ask your father later."
The girl pines for her crib, stowed away in back,
and she sighs for her favorite brother, left back in Ohio.

One child too many to come
and the uncle and aunt cherish him so, was the talk.
But so does she.

The train, puffing, thirsty dragon,
halts in a squat wooden town, Gothenburg.
Father and the wagon wait. Jennie steps off into eager arms.
He has a deep gaze for the wife, returned only in flashes,
and candy for the children.
Crib piled into the back of the wagon with the trunks and the boys.
She is nestled in a buffalo robe between Mary and Father on the box.
Father lets her touch the whip.
They easily ford the wide, shallow Platte River and head south.

They climb a plum-trimmed canyon and reach the bare Hi-Line.
No houses. No trees.

Sunset, and the white crib is carried
across the sod house threshold.
Horace himself planed that threshold, framed the windows.
He lifts Mary down. “Well?”
She strides to the door and lifts the latch.
Gleaming pine floors catch the fading light.
“Nice, Horace. I’m here,” is all she will give him.

Jennie leaps from the wagon still clutching the buffalo robe.
Red gold purple green the twilight scoops deep below the low hills.
Stars twinkle in the east.
The country rolls out like a carpet in a long run to the sky.
She spins on the short grass.
No one notices or chides.
She can see forever.

Christmas Oranges

The children were not to watch
as Father unloaded the snowcapped wagon.
Crates and bushels went straight to the cellar
and under an Indian blanket.

Father pocketed the key with a wink.
Jennie had to sit to keep breathing,
her hands trembling as she cracked the walnuts.

That evening candles clipped to the fir were lit.
Their dots of light graced the gingham bows, the popcorn strings,

and cast deep shadows in the parlor corners.
Atop the white tablecloth brought from Ohio,
turkey with stuffing, yams, and fruit pies crowded

the table, so everyone ate standing or in the parlor.
Mother fanned herself at the fire, exhausted, while
Nora the hired girl hovered, hiding homesick tears.
Family and neighbors joined in rolling up the rugs,
then with fiddles and dancing. Jennie missed the beat.

Stepping to the window, she gazed through the frosted panes.
Stars arched over the prairie. Horses stomped under their blankets.

Father called her into the kitchen.
"I want you to see these first, Jennie. Remember?"
His carpenter's hands, deft and hard, pried a crate open.
Golden spheres burned into view, sweet and strange.
"Oranges!" she cried. Father laughed, "They made the last train."
She remembered from last year to peel them first.
The flesh exploded in her mouth—
Ocean. Green. Warm. Sunshine.
She closed her eyes and swallowed. *Not here*, in one taste.

She carried a bowlful into the parlor.
The music stopped. The dancers paused.
She beamed as everyone surrounded her, each reaching for
an orange, the only one any of them would eat that year.
The night froze in her memory like crystals on the panes,
melting into a tale from time to time, like now,
for me, then freezing again for the next blue hour.

Cleveland Gallery

Robert had written as soon as he returned.
Brother Rollie had written, too.
"Come, Jennie" they both said. "Come to Ohio."
She sat at her sewing table and read each one.
She had tried to put Robert out of mind
when he'd gone back to Ohio that August.
She had even started up with nice Cal.
Now this.
There was money enough but no time . . . unless . . .
Mrs. Hancock was kind but older.
Her mending and making had slowed.
Customers knew Jennie's heart was not in it
by the way she cut the last threads too long, or not at all.
"She's too blind to see Jennie doesn't give a fig," was the wag.
Only a few knew where Jennie's heart really lay—Ohio.

"Jennie, I'm sorry, but I'm closing shop."
Mrs. Hancock's words cut through Jennie's dilemma.
"Time to cushion the needle, I say. Sorry, dear."
Jennie burst out laughing.
The kind old lady had no idea why.

Mrs. Hancock moved in with a sister back in Wisconsin.
Cal was of course happy to drive her to the train. Poor fool.
He polished the harness and got a new robe for the seat.
He leaned in for a kiss goodbye and she gave him a quick peck.
She hoped he wouldn't wait for her.

Sun was setting as the express to New York eased to a smoky stop.
After Chicago, Cleveland seemed only a little smaller,
still head-spinning to a small-town prairie girl.
She was the first out of the Pullman;
almost left her trunk on the train.
Robert and Rollie both stood on the platform in their stiff collars.
Rollie got a hug and a kiss.
Robert shook her hand for now. They kissed later, on the porch.
It was just as it had been at the last picnic on Medicine Creek.
She leaned into the wool of his shoulder. He drew her close.
She felt alive again. A misty future took shape.

The big house sat on a broad lawn.
And the trees, the trees!
Her prairie eyes marveled at the trees.
Aunt Martha gave her light chores—some baking, setting the table.
A maid and a cook did the rest.
Rollie's room was next to hers on the third floor.
He would sneak in and sit in her cane chair.
They giggled like they once had as children
until Uncle Hack's cane tapped up from below,
then whispered some more.
Jennie never laughed like this at home.

Martha took her downtown.
She dared the streetcar and found
she liked watching people, admiring houses
as the train glided down broad avenues of fall foliage.
They passed a storefront gallery.
There were only a few people viewing
paintings from the plein air season:
Presque Isle beaches, boats on Lake Erie,
dairy cows sinking in mud.
"Why paint mud?" sneered Aunt Martha.
"Because it's there," said a whiskered man, eyeing Jennie.
"Do you like my pictures?"
"I don't know. I've never seen one—"
"Jennie," snorted Martha, "of course you have."
"—with the painter in the room, I mean."
"Want to try it for yourself?"
Aunt Martha gave the man a glaring take.
"Yes, I would. Thank you," Jennie said.

She was told the north light was the best.
Brushes weren't needles, but good fingers helped just the same.
Turpentine and oils pinched her nose,
but the color, the color:
even mud was sublime if you mixed it right.
Nothing was as like as she wanted, at first,
but soon under her touch the canvas came alive,
landscapes especially. She could paint
snow on a mountain so cold it burned your nose;
you could breathe that pine air.
The whiskered man hovered and pointed.

She could smell his pomade.
She knew there was more to his attention, but she ignored all that.
Her starched shirtwaist and the combs in her hair never cracked.
Only her fingers took on the day's colors, then the week's,
unwashable as the glow in her eyes.

Robert gave her pictures a once-over.
He wasn't sure.
"I'll get better with practice," she smiled
"Hmmm. This is taking a lot of time," he mumbled.
He caught himself.
"It's good to see you're making the most
of your time here."
"My time here?"
She followed him out the door.
Mr. Whiskers looked down.

Aunt Martha threw a New Year's Eve party
December 31, 1899: a new century.
More chairs, more help, music, the house boomed with life.
Every lamp was lit.
Jennie put on a new dress someone else had made just for her.
She pinched her cheeks and looked in the mirror.
Would he? Tonight? A new century!
It would be such perfect timing.
She descended slowly down the stairs, her skirts lapping behind her.
Robert kissed her hand, glancing only a moment
at the paint-stained nails.
He filled her punch and they raised their crystal cups.
The whisky burned through the sugar as she swallowed, choked.

A platter of oranges caught her eye, then she looked at Robert again.
He was at the door, bowing to a feathered beauty in a jet-flecked shawl.
Rollie was at her side holding her arm.
"Well, well, Elizabeth Bow.
Hot Springs must not have worked out."
Robert and Jennie didn't dance even once.
Jennie lasted until midnight
and then vanished at the last stroke of twelve.
The new century had begun, not as expected.
She never drank alcohol again.

It was her coldest January.
She caught a flu and spent days in bed,
wrapped in blankets in the heatless room.
The cold and sick soothed her, somehow.
Aunt Martha asked no questions until one day,
"What will you do, Jennie?"
"I'm going back." She had just written to Cal.
"Why, dear? You know you can stay."
Jennie looked out the window at the heavy oak branches just outside.
"I need to see the sky again."

Before she returned she saw them in the Wade Oval.
They were driving in his carriage.
Lizzie Bow leaned back and waved her shawl, nonchalant.
Robert looked away.
Jennie gazed after them
as she stood by the frozen pool.
She didn't smile again until somewhere in Iowa.
The open spaces soothed her.

Maude had insisted she move in with her. She had no sooner
removed her hat when Maude said,
"Jennie, Cal is engaged to Sally Ricketts now."
"He never answered my letters."
"Now you know why. It's a bit distracting to be courting
the only daughter of the richest man in the county."
Jennie faltered.
"What's to become of me now?"
Maude made her a cup of tea.

Jennie set up her sewing machine in Maude's dining room.
A flake of vermillion lingered under a fingernail.
She lightened a little every time she saw it.
She ordered a set of paints and brushes
before she threaded a single needle.

Jennie Hicks, *The Elk in the Glade*, 1930's. Oil on Canvas.
23 x 17.5 in. Collection of Kent and Theresa Whitacre

The Elk in the Glade

Arthur was the son of an odd couple:
        a wounded Civil War veteran, Horatio, who had
        been languishing in a DC hospital when Lincoln was shot; and
Catherine, the belle of a defunct Philadelphia fortune.
        Her mother's father, Ripka, had come from Austria
        with a command of machine looms. He built
        a cotton mill in the 1830s and got rich.
        His daughter married into the Whitakers,
        descendants of British deserters who chopped wood for a living.
        But in two generations, a Whitaker daughter
        had married the governor of Pennsylvania.

All this glamour ended for Catherine's family with the Civil War.
Cotton was embargoed and the mill was closed, the family ruined.
They melted their last silver dollars into spoons
emblazoned with the initial *R*, for Ripka,
which Catherine carried in her portmanteau all the way to the Hi-Line.

Catherine and Horatio were sent West by her doctors.
The air might do her good.
The land officer seemed not to blink
when a man who could barely walk filed a homestead claim.

The move excited Horatio, who was eager to leave behind
stuffy Philadelphia with its aftermath of bankruptcy.
Catherine, a proper, demanding, sharp-tongued snob,
set an elevated tone for the whole family.
No sod house for her. She let Arthur
stay indoors and read his books
while blizzards howled outside their proper frame house.
Her mother's porcelain teacups lined the top shelf,
a constant dusting hazard to the succession of Irish hired girls.

Catherine's low opinion of Hi-Line girls had kept Arthur
single longer than Horatio thought proper.
Arthur taught country school and in summer
farmed Horatio's homestead for him. He drove a four-
wheeled trap and kept to himself.

Catherine needed a new dress for the GAR picnic.
Grand Army of the Republic. She hated this
sentimental, sometimes boozy gathering of veterans.
But her garrulous Horatio thrived on company and
the war had been his moment.
Even she could not bear to withhold one of his few pleasures.
Having heard good things, she called on Jennie,
who pumped her Singer at Maude's, where she boarded.
Jennie was one of the few girls in town not afraid of Catherine,
who reminded her of one or two hostesses she'd met in Cleveland.
Her traveled eye and straightforward manner reassured Catherine.
Jennie had been East. Jennie had taste.
She recommended a narrower skirt, no petticoat.

Catherine would think about it. She was about to leave
when her eye caught a picture hanging over the sewing machine:
it was an elk in a mountain glade, its majestic antlers pitched back,
its mouth open in a mating call.
"Where did you get this, Jennie? It's lovely."
Catherine's voice rang like a bell.
"A friend gave it to me."
"Really? Who? Someone in town?"
Jennie blushed. "Hmmm. I have to confess,
ma'am, I painted it myself. Just dabbling on my own account—"
Catherine's eyes narrowed. "Never sell yourself short, dear."

That night, as Brigid cleared dishes from the pot roast
and Horatio pushed his wheelchair back and lit his pipe,
Catherine glanced at Arthur.
"That Jennie . . ." her voice trailed off.
The men leaned in, waiting for the barb.
". . . is doing a nice job on my dress."
Arthur nodded. Horatio blew out a blue puff.
"She might be worth asking to the GAR picnic."
"Really?" Arthur coughed and opened his book.
He pretended to read.
Nothing more was said about it.
Later Catherine sat in bed tending to her hair.
Horatio wheeled in and, gripping the side table,
hoisted himself into bed beside her. This feat
had become mundane to them.
"Jennie, eh?" he asked with a grin.
"We'll see," said Catherine. "There's only so much a mother can do."

"And that's where you start in," he laughed.
"Horatio. Please."

Jennie opened her door expecting Cal's Sally,
a regular customer. (The smarting never faded.)
"Arthur?" They'd long forgotten how they'd met,
but they had hardly ever spoken.
"Jennie." He entered, hat in hand.
Jennie saw he wore a stiff collar.
His horse and trap were hitched at the post out front.

He must have left the farm work early and washed up.
Orphan spinster and bachelor stood in silence a moment.
"I would be honored if you would accompany me to the GAR, Jennie."
He looked at her with intense brown eyes, eyes much like her own.
Her business composure sagged.
She had not gone out with anyone since Cal.
"Well, I don't know. Sunday, is it?"
"Afternoon, along Medicine Creek.
They like to be in under the shade.
The food is okay if you don't mind the spiders and speeches.
No one goes on like an old soldier, and
here you have a few dozen all in one place."
Jennie smiled at how he went on. She noted his gaze.
She had not been looked at like that in a while.
"If you promise not to make me laugh
with your awful sarcasm, Arthur, okay, I'll go."
Arthur nodded. "Okay."

It was the kind of town that saw them
married as soon as it saw them together:
the picnic, Saturday nights strolling up and down Main Street
thronged with farmers and school kids;
a man and a woman in their mid-twenties,
she a little checkered, he a picky mamma's boy.
They both resisted the encouraging smiles,
the staged dinner invitations,
the not-so-invisible hand of Catherine,
who peppered the church ladies with
penciled notes that made more of the match than it was.
Arthur and Jennie called it *the campaign* and conspired
to thwart it. They staged a tiff at Becky Cleaver's.
He pretended to sulk after church.
She put on a breakfast mope for Maude to tell everyone about.

They bonded resisting the small-town fishbowl,
entertained themselves by their games
even as they began to see something more in each other.
They tricked themselves into becoming in fact the item
everyone else saw from the beginning.
Jennie struggled not to hope.
Maude kept saying Arthur was the bachelor type.
Jennie's stomach tightened every time Maude said it.
She wrote a school friend in Gothenburg
and asked to set up shop there if this didn't work out.
Farnam was getting very small.

She came home one day to find him
staring at her picture on the wall.
It was not the first time he'd opened the unlocked door.
"Sorry to intrude . . ."
"I saw your horse outside."
"Mother told me you painted."
"Yes, I guess I do."
He played with his hat. For once he seemed tongue-tied.
"It's a nice picture, Jennie."
"Thank you."
He looked at the floor.
"We could stop horsing around."
Now she looked down. "We could, I guess."
He looked up at her. "Not only is there almost no one else,
Jennie, there really is no one else. We shouldn't let them down."
She let out a laugh. "Oh, is that why?"
He backed away. "No! No! That's the joke, see?
That's what I'm saying we should move on from."
"To what?"
"You're making me say it, aren't you?"
"You're so good with words, Arthur."
He took her hand. He spoke. She nodded.
They were well into uncountable kisses
when Maude banged through the door.
"That horse needs water, Arthur. Oh—?"
She let out a little laugh. Jennie smiled at her.
"Well, I guess you can too make them drink," Maude said.

Catherine came by the next day.
She gave Jennie a formal hug. "Bless you, Jennie.
You have a mother again," she warbled,
her usual clarion voice caught for some reason.
"Thank you, ma'am." Jennie's voice trembled a little, too.
"Please. Mother."
"Mother."
"Now, for the wedding . . ."
They sat down under the picture,
and Jennie listened as her new life unfolded.

Cassandra in the Depression

The Great Depression devoured the Hi-Line. It chewed up banks. It swallowed the rain. It blew the soil into roving clouds. It pried loose and rolled West anyone who wasn't bolted to the plow, including Jennie's younger brother, Loren, who moved his family to Seattle.

The 1930s started with men heading every household in the family. In a few years half would be gone, in a sequence of events Jennie's oldest daughter, Esther, foretold. She was cursed with that gift, our Cassandra.

The eldest daughter, they could not agree on her name. So, names were scribbled on slips of paper and placed in a bowl. The baby pulled out Esther, rather than Arthur's choice, Isabelle, which became her middle name. He never called her anything but Daughter.

Esther was a typical older sister—direct, bossy sometimes, and from early years eager for people and adventure. She not only ran with the gang; she ran the gang. She and Arthur forged a deep, essential bond. He could tell her things he told no one else, including Jennie, so busy, so moody sometimes.

Esther married Harlan, the love of her life and a bright light in Kearney: teacher, Boy Scout troop master. People had their eye on him. Soon they had a baby boy, my father. They were offered a post in Hawaii, where teachers were badly needed. Then one day Harlan was rushed to the hospital with appendicitis. He survived the operation just fine. He was only twenty-eight years old, after all. After a week of bed rest, not allowed to get up at all, he was ready to go home. Esther and Jennie went home to get lunch and were about to return for him when the phone rang.

"Mother, please get that. It's the hospital and Harlan has died."

Jennie had heard these kinds of things from Esther before. She walked to the phone and picked up the earpiece. It was the hospital. Indeed, Harlan was gone. He had sat up after a week flat on his back and pitched over with a stroke. Years later the doctor told Esther every time he saw her how much he regretted losing Harlan.

Mother and child moved in with Arthur and Jennie on the farm. Esther cried long into every night. They covered the child's crib with a sheet to keep out the dust. The boy would remember getting nauseous at the breakfast table watching Arthur pour cream on his pancakes. A couple of years passed. Esther opened a dress shop down the Hi-Line in Curtis. Ruth helped out. Down the street, a widower named Ferris ran the hardware store. Before long Esther and Ferris were eating lunch at the cafe. He proposed. She said yes. She and her son moved into his big white house by the park, where he and his daughter, Donna, had been making do since her mother died.

Arthur lost one farm but held on to the other one. The dry brown years would be remembered long after the rains finally returned and World War II lifted up the markets. But by then the farm life would be over for Arthur and Jennie.

Arthur still followed many of the Victorian traces from his mother. He used his initials, A. O., even in letters to his daughters. Mealtimes were adult times; children were to be seen and not heard. His shorthorns were prized when he sold them in Omaha. His instincts for weather and crops carried him through losses and drought. He had followed Jennie's whims, like moving to Kearney for the girls' schooling. He was glad when Esther remarried and got back on her feet.

Esther, Ferris, and the children came out for Sunday dinner. Arthur looked around the table with satisfaction: the aster-patterned china, a little boy and girl, smiling newlyweds, the prized ruby-red drinking glasses, a platter of roast beef. Jennie and Esther washed up. There was no hired girl these days, but times were getting better. They said their goodbyes and drove away. Arthur sat back in his chair to read, maybe Shakespeare, a novel, or the markets. Maybe Arthur napped.

Esther turned to Ferris as he pulled onto the main road. "I won't see Dad alive again," she said matter-of-factly.

He looked at her. He had never heard her talk like this. "Hope you're wrong."

"Me too."

The next day Arthur shoveled some muck from the barn into the manure spreader and hitched up the team. The bed of the spreader was a belt driven by the moving wheels that fed manure into a rotating beater at the back. The beater broke up the manure and dropped it onto the field, where it improved the soil. For a while now he had meant to buy a tractor-driven spreader and retire the two Belgian horses once and for all from this, their last purpose. But money was tight, and by now the Belgians pretty much drove themselves back and forth across the field, giving him a chance to daydream and think about his reading.

After about forty-five minutes, the belt had left a ridge of manure along the edges. He dropped the reins, crawled back into the box, straddled the moving belt, and started scraping while the horses plodded on. He was thinking about something he had heard at the co-op: selling his shorthorns on contract at a future date. It locked in the price, but if something happened to the calves you were on the hook . . . The world was getting back on its feet, and he wasn't sure prices would hold up. Germany seemed to be—

Something, no one ever knew what—a snake, a tumbleweed, a terror from a past life—startled the horses and they lunged into a trot, then a canter. Their speed was translated by the gears to the beater, which turned ever faster. Arthur fell forward into the manure and was hauled by the belt into the accelerating beaters. He took several hits to his head, lost an ear. It broke his back, punctured his kidneys, and then crushed his pelvis before he emerged from the mauling and fell to the unplowed ground. The stench and the slime were beyond his awareness. He lingered for weeks in agonized semiconsciousness before finally fading away, fifty-six years old.

The Belgians were lot #42 at the farm sale. They went for dog food and glue. No one trusted them or needed them. All along the Hi-Line the heavy collars and harnesses were being hung up in barns to molder while tractors were oiled for spring plowing. Years later, children playing in the hay would marvel at these old leather masterpieces, coated in dust and still smelling of Belgian sweat. Then the barns themselves would be pulled down and thrown into ravines or repurposed into hunting lodges, fancy restaurants, planters. The old harness hook now holds a hanging petunia in someone's breezeway.

And so Arthur and Jennie missed the wet, good years of World War II and its aftermath, when those who lasted became millionaires and their grandchildren became yuppies and MBAs. Just so, Harlan and Esther had missed the golden ring of Hawaii, with its skyrocketing land values and surging, war-driven growth. These two deaths would echo down through the family for generations.

Esther's clairvoyance would become a family legend. There was the time when a plane flew overhead in Curtis and she knew her ten-year-old son was on board it. Indeed, he had stumbled across some airmen while wandering around town with his buddies, and they had taken them up for a joyride.

Or there was Mother's Day my senior year, when she had a bad feeling as soon as we said goodbye. Later that week I rolled a car on a county bridge and could easily have been killed. But I escaped untouched. She said she felt better after that day was over and she hadn't heard that anything had happened. Even the last time I saw her alive in the nursing home, we looked into each other's eyes and we both knew this was our last time together. Tears welled as we hugged goodbye as we had never hugged before.

Then, the night of the day she died, I was trying to sleep in my New York apartment when I heard a crash in the kitchen. A fire extinguisher had flown off the wall. I knew she was saying goodbye.

Back in 1936, after the farm sale, Jennie watched as the girls and their husbands packed her things. There was a little white house in town she'd had her eye on, and now it was hers. She went upstairs and took one item off the upper shelf of the spare room closet: her box of paints.

You never know, she thought, unless you're Esther.

Gillette

Ruth, her lovely youngest, red haired like the
best of her family, nearly died in high school.
And though she survived she would never bear
children. Her Romeo, the love of her life,
fled, and in came Glen, an awkward, stuttering boy
raised on a Sand Hills ranch.

He takes her to their new homestead in Gillette, Wyoming.
The truck bounces up the ruts to the
homestead shack. There is her mother-in-law,
Mary, wringing clothes by hand over a tub.
"Son, tell the wife the dough is ready," is the welcome.
Ruth keeps the prayer book she'd brought as a gift.

Ruth shades her eyes against the blazing sun of the high range.
A ridge of buttes notches the horizon,
the shore of a sea of sand-blown scrub.
She wants to swim away from the penal colony air
Mary and Glen breathe in that rattling shack.
They speak only to give her more work.

She was the best friend in school, best dresser, best dancer.
Her flapper hands harden; her freckles merge into a tan.
Hunched over the oilcloth-covered table, they eat
from the shriveled garden her labors cannot coax.
Thin walls, and Mary knows what is not happening at night.
Blaming looks over chicory coffee next morning.

"How are the beans, girl?" "They're already dead."
"I told you to water them." "You planted them in rocks."
"Glen, see how she talks to me?"
Ruth stifles a thousand retorts that she pours into letters home.
Drought and falling prices heighten the gloom.
She wanders the bluffs, resenting the free-ranging antelope.

Glen's horse goes missing. He knows where it is.
"Them Stiller boys took it." Their rancher neighbor was
full of mischief: fences cut, cattle driven through the wheat.
"Then go get it back." Her brown eyes charge him
as never before. Glen has to look away. But he pulls
on his boots and starts out on foot ten miles to the ranch.

He walks up to the barn. His horse whinnies to him
from the corral. A cowboy threatens he'll shoot if he touches it.
Glen says not one word. He opens the gate, slips on the bridle
he had brought, mounts up, and rides bareback past the cowboy.
He would become a legend among the dirt farmers,
who have little else to celebrate as they eke out the '30s.

Glen returns with his horse and a rare smile.
Mary runs out; she can hardly contain her awe.
"What made you think you could do that, son?"
Ruth stands aside, arms folded. "I told him to."
Mary's face falls. She walks inside. The screen door slams.
At supper Ruth tells a story. Glen laughs. Mary is a cloud.

In the new year word comes that it's so bad
the government will buy them out, revert the land to range.
Then Father writes them about a place on the Hi-Line:
a two-story well-built house in a little valley
at the end of a wandering lane, eight hundred acres,
pastures and fields, and five minutes from Farnam.

Ruth takes the letter to Glen in the fields.
He strokes the gaunt flanks of the hungry horse.
Mary is stalking toward them, fists clenched.
"I can't be stuck anymore between you two women."
"Stuck? Glen, you never stood up for me once.
Sell. Or I go back alone."
"Then you tell Mother."

She turns. Her look stops Mary in her tracks.
They ship what they have, a couple of horses,
some scrawny cows, a shovel, and a plow,
back to the Hi-Line and settle down. Home.
Forty-five years later, when they sell up,
many cows would be descended from Gillette stock.

Mary stayed on a few more years.
But even she couldn't last long
and died alone during the war.

No, they would never forget Gillette.
Between a horse and a husband, they had each
learned to grab what they needed and keep moving.

Bombing with Ruth

I have been sent out to help Uncle Glen with the fencing.
Our mornings are spent in the milkweed and thistle
wrestling posts into the ground and stringing barbed wire
that we jack into place at each corner until it twangs.
The work is hard, in spurts, but Glen is easy company.
He appreciates the help of a teenage nephew.
But I am eager to join Jennie's daughter, my aunt Ruth,
for an afternoon bombing around the county in her Plymouth.

My aunt Ruth has a ready laugh and a soft voice.
Her dancing eyes hold a smile like no other.
She and her Plymouth are well known, as she flies
from church circle to Farm Bureau to funeral to coffee.
She's a ranch wife in her prime. The cellar shelves groan
under the weight of bushels she has canned: peaches, beans, pickles.
She's famous for her pies, though she swears she just follows
the standard recipe for her crusts:
flour, water, shortening, each ingredient half of the prior one.
(But I still think she took a secret on this subject to the grave.)
Come pheasant season Ruth's table
stretches to welcome family and friends—
Texas millionaires, Hungarian refugees from the hell of '55,

my dad, me, and my brother. We stalk Glen's shelter belts
and milo fields for lavish ring-necked pheasants.
By afternoon the birds are lined up for a photo with the dogs
and the cistern head is gory from the day's dressing.

Ruth's memory holds more than she could ever tell.
How she does regale. A plume of dust trails,
our ups and downs and lazy turns on the pink gravel roads that
shoot between ditches of rattlesnakes and ground squirrels,
in and out of shallow clay-banked canyons dotted
by yucca and a struggling tree or two.

The sky is blue and vast, like the stories
that pour and pour, with laughter,
awe, and that winning smile:
a strange loner, feeding threshing crews,
the batty aunts, the tonsillectomy they gave her on
the dining room table, cauterized
by hot spoons down the throat.
Even a lynching.

We come home to apple pie at her kitchen table
as the afternoon sun slants past the twin cottonwood trees
into the south windows, past the geraniums.
The big white barn casts shadows across the yard.
I know an old harness hangs in one of the stalls.

Decades later I come into her room at the home.
She lies on her back, smiling her own smile.
"How are you, Ruth?"
"Fine, fine." She speaks through closed eyes. "I'm remembering.
When you were boys . . . what a time!"
She opens her eyes.
For once neither of us can say more.

The Neighbor with the Saber

He arrived in Farnam quietly and kept to himself,
a skinny, cigar-smoking fellow with crystal-blue eyes
that never looked you square.
No one knew if he'd bought or rented the old Russell place.
But he seemed to know
the working end of a plow okay.
He managed for himself, somehow;
never hired a girl or anything.
Sally Rickets even saw him out
hanging laundry one day.
She laughed with a snort every time she told of it.
"Why, whoever thought a MAN would do that?"
Sally herself thought later how, of course,
soldiers do their own wash.

There were other clues.
When no one had seen him for a few days, Bill Cleaver
knocked on his door. He was met by a wheezing,
sweaty ghost railing at him with a saber,
his greasy hair long and scraggly as his beard.
His gibberish was incomprehensible but

his eyes looked like he'd seen hell.
People left him alone after that.

Sheets blew in the wind for a while.
But then his plow horse showed up at the Cleavers.
Its ribs stuck out like jail bars across its side.
It was the bawling of the unmilked cow
that brought Bill Cleaver back to the paint-chipped porch.
No answer to his knock, he walked in.
He found him on the bed, hands folded across his belly,
eyes fixed on a ceiling stain.
A mouse or something had started in on his nose.
But what struck Bill was what he had on:
the blue full-dress uniform of the Seventh Cavalry,
Custer's brigade of infamous repute.
And his saber lay by his side,
properly fastened to his belt.
He wore his white gloves.
"Ready for his last stand," Bill later said.

Was he a deserter? A survivor?
They talked about it for years.
Bill would never forget those gaping eyes
as he gazed upon that full-dress corpse.
Those eyes had seen things:
horses tumbling dead onto their riders,
waking under a pile of bodies,
knives circling skulls for the scalp,
crawling away in the night
leaving carnage behind, but not ever.

Had he even been at Little Big Horn that historic day?
There was no note, no letter,
just enough silver dollars in a cigar box
to bury him in the Farnam Cemetery
with his mysteries and full military honors.

Coming to the White House

Jennie wanted the library table in front
of the south window.
A new propane stove barely fit in the kitchen at the back.
Her bedroom suite of golden maple
brightened the north bedroom.
Her plaster bust of a child reading
caught the light nicely
as she sat in her special chair at the end of the day,
alone.

The electric light glared.
It would be a while before she trusted it
enough to put away the kerosene lamps.
There was no outhouse,
so she hoped the toilet would be reliable.
It would be nice come winter, she remembered,
from the years in Kearney putting the girls through school.
So much had changed in Farnam
since her days sewing in Maude's house.
So many people had left in the hard times,
or had died: Horatio, Catherine, Maude.
They were bringing her a radio.

But tonight loomed empty and she felt
alone alone alone.

She walked into the kitchen,
washed a dish,
folded a towel.
Then she opened the pantry door.
There on the table, the only furniture in the room,
was her box of paints.
A roll of canvas leaned against the wall.
She took out her tape measure and scissors
and began to prep.

A few days later Ruth stopped by with her friend Gladys.
They found Jennie in one of Arthur's old shirts,
the pantry wall lined with three paintings:
a mountain cabin, a howling wolf, a cowboy on horseback
fighting through a blizzard to make his log cabin in the night.
"Mother!" Ruth beamed. "Will you look at this."
Gladys paused in the door.
"Jennie? My land, I had no idea!"
Jennie smiled. "Do you like them?"
"Oh, yes, I sure do."
"Which is your favorite?"
"The cowboy. Yep. The cowboy."
"That's a nice one, Mother," Ruth held it up.
"You can have it then, Gladys."
"Oh, Jennie, no."
"Yes. Please. What am I going to do with it?
I just paint these to pass the time now that—well . . ."

The women paused.
It has been such a short time, really, since . . .
"Jennie, I'll talk to Harold. I would like to have it, I guess.
But I'll pay you for it. How much?"
"No, no, please."
"Now, now. How much?"
Jennie shrugged. "Oh, a couple of dollars?"
"Mother, I think you mean five dollars."
Gladys smiled. "Yes, that's about right. Five dollars."
Jennie shook her head but said nothing.

Gladys came back the next day,
took the cowboy home. Another picture
lined the pantry wall by then.
"Jennie, you don't have to go back to sewing.
People will want these."
"You think so?"
"Ruth and I can get the word out. You'll see."

Soon the white house had a steady traffic
and Jennie was in the picture trade.
Two or three pictures sold a week:
mountain landscapes, wildlife, horses.
She copied prints, calendars, postcards
and charged by size.
She was a seamstress who sewed in oils
to a pattern, often on demand.
Her colors and brushstrokes were compelling.
And the lush landscapes brightened
newly electrified farm homes that looked out

on featureless horizons,
though the brilliant skies at sunset
could mirror her canvas peaks.

Evenings she would sit on her porch
in her big wicker chair as people passed by.
She was not yet sixty, her family raised,
done for good with farm chores, free.
Her pictures would wind up in forty-eight states,
a couple of foreign countries.
She would take the train to Ohio, to Rollie, a couple more times.
She would be interviewed on the radio.
The paper would write a story about her.
Grandma Moses would write to her.
This would do. She became herself.

Jennie Hicks, *Esther's Mountain Meadow*, 1951. Oil on canvass, 50.5 x 39.5 in. Collection of Mark and Renae Whitacre.

Dorathy in the Middle

An almost Irish twin to Esther's alpha,
barely older than flirty, red-headed Ruth,
Dorathy middled and soothed almost unseen
until she married Kronberg, the Great Dane.
They settled on good Platte River land,
daughter of the long-distance call, safe it seemed
from early widowhood or a mismatched marriage.

It was the good years: Depression done, war prices for corn.
But her third child, Denny, born more than colicky,
cried so hard he herniated and passed out.
When he came to he was never the same.
Heart of gold, but *simple* was maybe the polite word.
His frustrations and failures rallied the family to cope
with the daily crises of their stricken little boy.

The other three children moved on to college,
ranch, coasts, and mountains. But Denny
stayed on and stayed on. His parents
could find no place for him but theirs.

Dorathy's sad smile and welling eyes, the haunted look
she never lost, presided over ever-busy hands

canning, sewing, gardening, cooking . . .
keep going, keep doing, keep going.

She made time to take up her mother's brush
and became the best painter of the three daughters.
Animals were her specialty. Her five-kitten masterpiece
was so in demand she painted it many times.

The cherished pets she painted from Polaroids
and snapshots—the good hunter, the family mutt,
all those kittens—were each a life she could fix
in oil and canvas and send out into the world.

She knew a picture was not a child.
But sometimes light and color can fill in, just a little.

Pink

Jennie shuffles through the file of pictures
she clips from calendars and magazines:
a horse with a robin, a fly fisherman wading a river,
a country road passing a stone cottage,
two wolves howling in the night.
They will each make a fine painting.

She puts on an old shirt.
She mixes colors on the palette:
primary, white, turpentine.
She chooses a fine brush to mottle the snow
that caps the gray mountains at dawn:
red, white, turpentine.
A sip of coffee, and then
she is back on a train with Arthur
that honeymoon morning in Colorado.
The mountain ridge fades into distance:
white and more white, paler, paler pink.
It blushes the sky just enough.
His lips on her hand, her surprise.
She had never imagined such beauty,
and here was Arthur, her reason, her witness.

Another tunnel and the view is gone.
But she has captured it here once again,
as she will hundreds of times over dozens of years
in the small white house in the small town,
not quite alone.

Pride at the Shore

Serene
water barely ripples
as the she lion crouches to drink,
watched over by her dark-maned king.

Sublime
setting sun glazes the rocky cliff behind them,
lake ablaze in twilight,
last light before the hunt.

The picture of two lions painted by Jennie
at the birth of my father, her first grandchild,
floated with the river of the seven houses
in seventeen years—my youth in one town—
until it became home itself.
The stalwart couple, lion and lioness,
presided from rec room to bedroom
to mantle, when there was one,
its orange glow our constant hearth.
They were household deities,
a portrait of our parents' marriage,
a shrine to wild hearts in still moments.

Hard to square their menace and power
with the fragile farmwife who made them.
I believe their claws raked
something in her confined;
their pause slaked her own thirst, and ours,
before the hunt.

Jennie Hicks, *The Lions*, 1934. Oil on canvas, 25.75 x 19.75 in. Collection of Kent and Theresa Whitacre

To the Mountains

My high school and college years paralleled
Jennie's move from the white house.
She could no longer see to cover the canvas.
She forgot to empty the ashes in the stove.
She sometimes didn't hear to answer the phone.
Her daughters told her it was time.
She resisted, then surrendered
what she had finally won
all those years ago: freedom.

The white house was broken up—
a table to this grandchild,
pictures to these, Arthur's books to those,
the bust of the reading child to a niece.
Farnam had little left to hold her.
She had outlived all her friends.
She had begun to yearn to die.
She moved to a home in Kearney,
where a roommate blasted the heat
so much she couldn't sleep. Then to one in Curtis,
where one thing and then another for a half dozen years until,
almost ninety-eight, she passed on at last in 1977.

She had always said if she survived March, she'd last another year.
Not this time.
Held on a cold clear April day, grass green, trees about to bud,
the funeral was small, mostly the daughters with their matching
brown eyes, mirrors of her own, and their broods.
Jennie was eased into her place beside Arthur,
who had been waiting more than forty years.

Ruth and Esther would leave the Hi-Line soon themselves:
to Kearney, near where Dorathy had lived since marriage.
The white house proved to have no foundation
and was razed a few years later, its land blending into
the carpet of vacant lots of shrinking Farnam.

Jennie had never painted the prairie, the canyons,
or the majestic skies she called home all this time.
Her eyes had been on the mountains and lakes
she had seen herself so rarely but remembered
from that train to Portland.

Farnam Cemetery

Terrain so long unseen in
the swallowed void of life lived elsewhere
arises as the car surmounts the cedar-studded valley rim.
I am back at last on the Hi-Line after sudden decades.
How little a July cornfield changes over time.
Scan the vast horizon and it could be then again.

Only one frail cousin lingers
out on the family farm.
No one else left would know who we are
as we cruise past the empty lots of Main Street
where Jennie and Arthur strolled in Saturday night crowds
among a dozen stores.
The trains are long gone, half the people too.
Grain bins still rise near
the bare lot where once the white house stood.

The cemetery strides up the slope to the south,
busier every day.
And here they all still are—
Horace, Mary, Horatio, Catherine,
Esther, Harlan, Ruth, Glen, Arthur,
Jennie.

And so many more with the family names lie
under the granite and the buffalo grass,
where it is still Thanksgiving, Christmas, hunting season
and the stories are still passed around like mystery casserole,
repeated, stretched, contradicted,
then folded away until the next blue hour.
The good times buried here,
and the losses, the regrets, the blames,
anchor what I've been and where I've gone.
It is only a while yet
before I take my seat at the table
and pass on a tale.

Acknowledgements

"Christmas Oranges" was published by Poets Wear Prada in the Rainbow Project, December 2020.

My thanks to my brothers and their wives—Mark, Renae, Kent, and Theresa Whitacre—for allowing this book to include images of Jennie's pictures. To Arlene Unruh, one of Jennie's grandchildren, for sharing memories of painting with her. To Peg Boley, Jennifer Brown, Marianne Kindsfater, Ray and Sandi Kjar, Jodi Nelson, Jack Peck, Larry Unruh, Cheyenne Unruh, Doris Whitacre, and all the extended branches of the Hicks/Fitch family in Nebraska and beyond for holding the legacy of Jennie's paintings.

Special thanks to Crystal Werger and Cheri Bergman at the Dawson County Historical Society Museum, to Thomas Reese Gallagher and his colleagues at the Museum of Nebraska Art, Nicole Herden and Karissa Johnson, for their interest in Jennie's paintings.

Thanks to Lynn McGee for urging me to take on Jennie's story and for reading various drafts. Thanks to Brady Kelso for a very helpful early read of the manuscript. I am grateful to Roxanne Hoffman of Poets Wear Prada for publishing "Christmas Oranges" and for her support and advice in putting this book together. Thanks to Ladette Randolph and Patty Scarborough for their support. And thanks to all the poets who have taught and advised me and workshopped my poems over the years.

Portions of the proceeds of this book support arts education in rural Nebraska.

Land Acknowledgement

This book takes place and was written on unceded traditional lands of the Arapaho, Cheyenne, Maspeth, Matinecock, and Pawnee. The territories currently known as southwest Nebraska and central Queens, New York, originate from the Indigenous population that once inhabited these areas within Turtle Island. The Arapaho, Cheyenne, and Pawnee met with the US government in the 1860s. The Maspeth and Matinecock met with the Dutch and British in the 1600s.

Let this **land acknowledgment** be the beginning of a return to unity, not just of each other but also to the awareness that we are truly a part of the earth. Let us now walk with the knowledge that each and every one of us is a guardian of most importance, as **we were put upon this Turtle Island not to seek dominion but as caretakers**, as two-leggeds, to protect and to grow each other, to love and offer kindness. We are here to ensure that the gifts of earth, water, and air remain pure and whole, and so let us be guardians of the earth, the water, and the air, the four-legged, the fliers, the swimmers, the crawlers, the mammal people, and the green. In this way we honor the land that gives us life, we honor the lives and culture forsaken, and we honor the prospect of renewed alliances.

Moreover, let this moment of recognition be a monument of action. Action that is fortified with a cooperative spirit and reverence for traditional ways. Let it be the beginning of hope for this, our Turtle Island in the lands of the Arapaho, Cheyenne, Maspeth, Matinecock, and Pawnee.

Let us now stand, lifting our humanity, enrapturing with the earth's consciousness as guardians of harmony and kindness, as we pay respect to all our ancestors and to future generations.

About the Author

Bruce E. Whitacre was born and raised in Nebraska. His poems have appeared in *Big City Lit*, *Journal of American Poetry*, *World Literature Today*, and others, as well as the anthology *I Wanna Be Loved by You: Poems on Marilyn Monroe* and the craft book *The Strategic Poet*. This is his first book of poetry. www.brucewhitacre.com

CPSIA information can be obtained
at www.ICGtesting.com
Printed in the USA
LVHW081408251022
731527LV00010B/395